Charlie Chowdahead
Travels Boston

Ryan Gormady
Illustrated by Brian Daigle

Today, Charlie is traveling to Boston, one of the oldest cities in the country. Charlie is excited for the day ahead. With a map as his guide, he is ready to start his adventure!

To get around Boston, Charlie will ride America's oldest subway, known by locals as "The T." The conductor announces the name of each station. Listen closely Charlie, or you will miss your stop!

A great way to tour the city is on a duck boat. Half boat, half tour bus, they can travel by land or sea. Get ready to make quacking noises and find out more about the history of Boston!

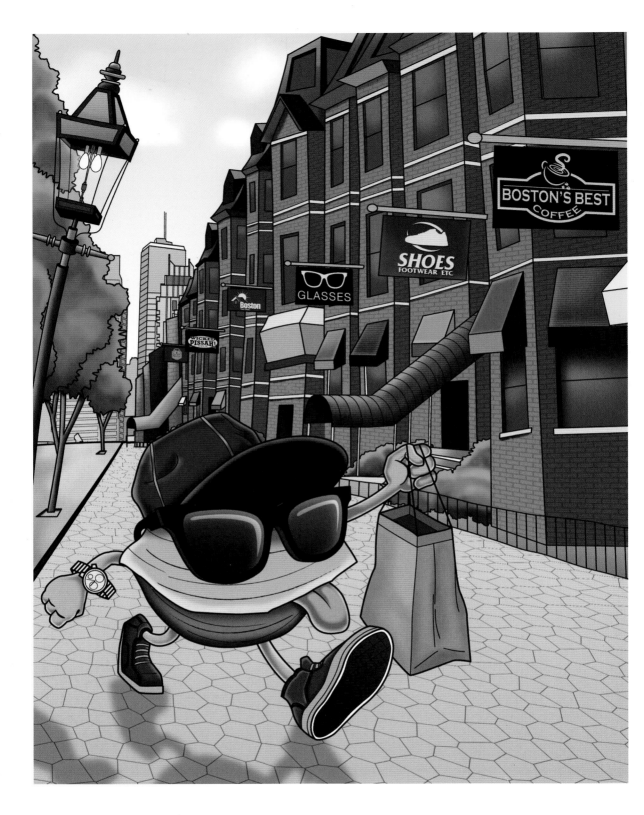

Charlie uses his map to find Newbury Street. With many great restaurants and stores, this is a hip spot to go shopping. Charlie picks up some cool shades and a shiny new watch, then he's off to the next stop on his tour.

"Wow," says Charlie, "it's the statue of Samuel Adams, a legendary patriot and one of the founding fathers of the United States." Located right in front of the famous Faneuil Hall, this is the perfect place for Charlie to stop and take a photograph!

Quincy Market is always full of eager tourists and locals looking for a bite to eat or a souvenir. Charlie is hungry from all this traveling, so he grabs a snack. "Mmmm," says Charlie, "this ice cream is delicious!"

Hooray! Charlie has made it to Fenway Park, the country's oldest baseball stadium and home of the Red Sox! Charlie is ready to sing "Take Me Out to the Ballgame" and eat a yummy hot dog. Hopefully, he will see the Sox win!

Charlie loves football, so he heads down to Foxboro to play with his favorite team, the New England Patriots. Look at Charlie go out for a pass and score a touchdown!

Charlie heads out for a walk on the Freedom Trail.
"Look! There is the statue of Paul Revere, Boston's
most famous messenger!" boasts Charlie.

It's time to stop for some pizza in the North End, an area of Boston known for its Italian-American heritage. Hey Charlie, don't forget to save room for dessert at one of the delicious bakeries!

After all that tasty food, Charlie needs some more exercise. Boston is home to one of the most famous marathons in the world. At 26.2 miles, it takes a lot of determination to finish this race! With a giant burst of energy, Charlie conquers "Heartbreak Hill." Charlie becomes the first clam ever to win the Boston Marathon! Way to go, Charlie!

After the big race, Charlie wants to go relax by the water. He takes a tour of the U.S.S. Constitution, the world's oldest floating naval vessel. It was nicknamed "Old Ironsides" during the War of 1812 because of the iron frame inside the ship's hull. Because of this special hull, enemy cannonballs bounced right off the ship!

Charlie isn't afraid to gear up and help the hometown hockey team, the Boston Bruins. "Check out my slap shot!" says Charlie. He shoots, he scores!

The people at the arena change the floor from an ice rink to a basketball court, so Charlie takes off his skates and laces up his basketball shoes. Charlie can jump pretty high for a clam. The crowd cheers as Charlie goes up for a slam dunk to win the game for the Celtics!

Charlie isn't just good at sports, he is also wicked smart and loves to learn new things. He makes his way to the Museum of Science, where they have lots of cool exhibits about plants, animals, outer space and electricity. Be careful Charlie, or you might get zapped!

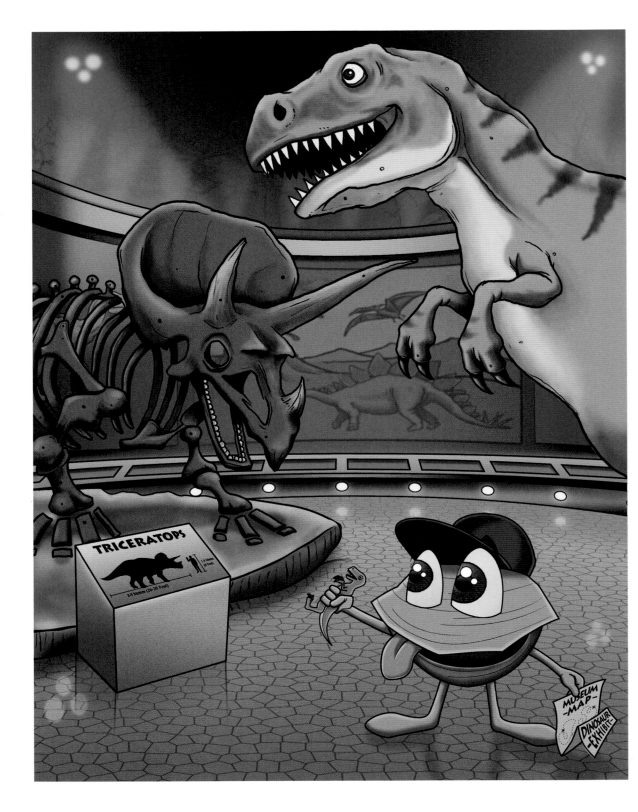

"I love the dinosaur exhibit. I just hope they don't come alive. Do any of these dinosaurs eat clams?" asks Charlie.

It's getting late, but Charlie has one more stop on his journey tonight. Charlie loves to listen to the Boston Pops at the "Hatch Shell" on the Charles River. This is also a great place to watch the fireworks on the 4th of July. With so much history, Boston is a great place to celebrate our nation's independence.

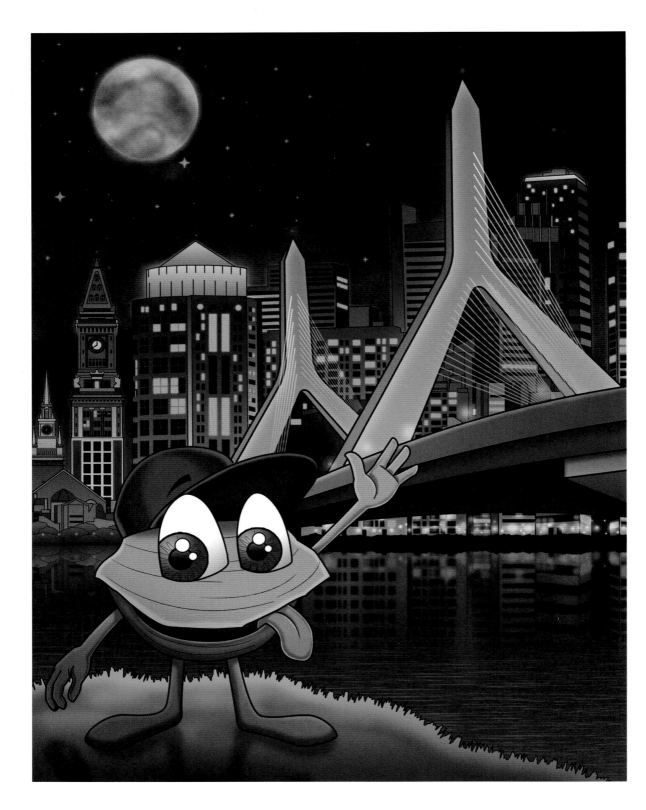

After a great day traveling around the city of Boston, Charlie waves good night to the Zakim Bridge and beautiful city skyline. Charlie had a wonderful time in Boston today. "Wow," says Charlie, "I can't wait for my next big adventure!"

The End

Visit Chowdaheadz.com for more Charlie Chowdahead products &

unique merchandise designed for Chowdaheadz of all ages

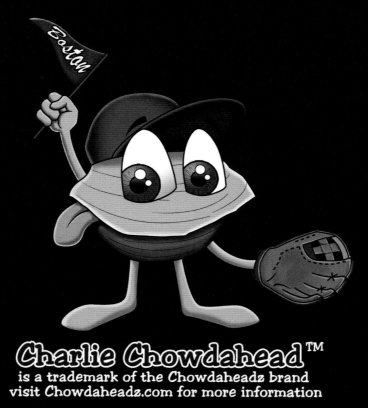

Charlie Chowdahead™
is a trademark of the Chowdaheadz brand
visit Chowdaheadz.com for more information

This book is dedicated to every Chowdahead
out there both young and old.

Special Thanks To: Susan Gormady, Brendan Hayes, Susan Fitzgerald, The Chowdaheadz Staff, & Friends

Share something with Charlie!

Send Charlie a message about your experience with this book, what it means to be a Chowdahead, or maybe about a trip you had to Boston.

We may post it on our blog, social sharing websites, or maybe even include it in a future book!

Email: charlie@chowdaheadz.com

Keep in Touch With Charlie!

Shop for Charlie Merchandise:
www.chowdaheadz.com

Join Charlie On Facebook:
www.facebook.com/chowdaheadz

Follow Charlie On Twitter:
www.twitter.com/chowdaheadz

Watch Charlie On Youtube:
www.youtube.com/chowdaheadz

Email Charlie:
charlie@chowdaheadz.com

www.mascotbooks.com

For more information, please contact Mascot Books, P.O. Box 220157, Chantilly, VA 20153-0157

ISBN: 1-936319-17-9
CPSIA Code: PRT0810A

Printed in the United States